This igloo book belongs to:

....

igloobooks

Published in 2019
by Igloo Books Ltd
Cottage Farm
Sywell
NN6 0BJ
www.igloobooks.com

0819 001.01
2 4 6 8 10 9 7 5 3 1
ISBN 978-1-78905-673-0

Written by Melanie Joyce
Illustrated by Katya Longhi

Designed by Stephanie Drake
Edited by Vicky Taylor

Printed and manufactured in China

The Yeti
who came to stay

igloobooks

Once, Billy read a story that was exciting and a little bit scary, about a creature called a yeti, who was

smelly, tall and **hairy.**

No one had ever seen it. They said it could **never** be found,
because all it left behind were footprints on the ground.

"Can we search for the yeti?" Billy begged his dad one day.

"Oh, alright," said Dad, with a sigh. "If you really insist.
But I have to tell you honestly, I don't think yetis exist."

Billy packed his backpack
and set off with his dad.

"Have fun," said his mum, waving,
thinking their plan quite mad.

They sailed across the sea,
took a train and rode on a bus.

Ding! Ding! went the bell.

Dad said, "This is the stop for us."

At the top of a mountain, they found footprints in the snow.

"Follow me," Billy said to Dad.

"I know which way to go."

At last they found the yeti. He was huge and covered in fur.
"What's your name?" asked Billy. The yeti answered,

"Urgh!"

"Urgh's a lovely name," said Billy.
"I'm very pleased to meet you."

But it's freezing here.
I want to go home.
Why don't you come, too?

"Urgh!" replied the yeti, smiling.
Billy took that as a 'yes'.

But what the yeti really said was anybody's guess.

Back home, Mum was shocked and said,

Oh dear, goodness me.
I hadn't really thought about
what a yeti might eat for tea!

The yeti ate pretty much everything, even Brussels sprouts and peas.

He didn't use a knife and fork, or say 'excuse me', 'thank you', or 'please'.

Billy didn't mind that his new friend **slobbered** and **Slurped**, or that he snored at night, smelled awful and often **burped**...

... because the yeti was so much fun.
He just wanted to play.

He didn't really understand
why people kept running away.

The days passed by so happily
and the two friends played together.

They loved to go exploring...

... and stayed out in all weather.

The yeti chased after Billy and bounced on the trampoline.

"Whoo-hoo!"
shouted Billy, giggling.

It was the **highest**
he'd ever been.

The yeti smiled all the time, until one night it began to snow.

"He's missing his home," said Mum.
"It's time for him to go."

So the yeti went back home. Billy felt lonely every day.
He really missed his friend and wished he hadn't gone away.

Then, one morning in the mail,
a postcard dropped on the mat.

'Urgh!' was all it said
and only a yeti would write that.

urgh!

So Billy packed his suitcase and went to visit his best friend.
And he was very sure, their friendship would never end.